Killing Time

ALSO BY ALAN BENNETT

plays

PLAYS ONE
(*Forty Years On, Getting On,*
Habeas Corpus, Enjoy)
PLAYS TWO
(*Kafka's Dick, The Insurance Man, The Old Country,*
An Englishman Abroad, A Question of Attribution)
THE LADY IN THE VAN
OFFICE SUITE
THE MADNESS OF GEORGE III
THE WIND IN THE WILLOWS
THE HISTORY BOYS
THE HABIT OF ART
PEOPLE
HYMN *and* COCKTAIL STICKS
ALLELUJAH!

television plays

ME, I'M AFRAID OF VIRGINIA WOOLF
(*A Day Out, Sunset Across the Bay, A Visit from Miss Prothero,*
Me, I'm Afraid of Virginia Woolf, Green Forms,
The Old Crowd, Afternoon Off)
ROLLING HOME
(*One Fine Day, All Day on the Sands, Our Winnie, Rolling Home,*
Marks, Say Something Happened, Intensive Care)
TALKING HEADS
TWO BESIDES

Alan
Bennett

Killing Time

First published in 2024
by Faber & Faber Ltd
The Bindery, 51 Hatton Garden
London EC1N 8HN
and
Profile Books Ltd
29 Cloth Fair, London EC1A 7JQ

Typeset by Agnesi Text, Hadleigh, Suffolk
Printed and bound by CPI Group (UK) Ltd, Croydon CRO 4YY

A CIP record for this book is available from the British Library

ISBN 978-0-571-39481-4

MIX
Paper | Supporting
responsible forestry
FSC® C171272

Printed and bound in the UK on FSC® certified paper in line with our continuing
commitment to ethical business practices, sustainability and the environment.
For further information see faber.co.uk/environmental-policy

2 4 6 8 10 9 7 5 3 1

Killing Time

'Hello? Hill Topp House? Am I speaking to Mrs McBryde?'

'No.'

'Who am I speaking to?'

'Nobody. Audrey. I live here.'

'Is Mrs McBryde there?'

'No. There's nobody here. The door was open. I was passing.'

'Perhaps you should put the phone down and then I can call back and leave a message?'

'We're not supposed to answer the phone, only I thought it might be for me.'

'No.'

'I can take a message. I was good at that. It's what I used to do. For Mr Firbank. Ellis and Firbank, Solicitors, on Drummond Street. He's dead, Mr Ellis.

Mr Firbank was always the main man. Was it him you were wanting?'

'No. I just want some information. Thank you. I'll call back.'

She rang off.

'Hello? Hello?'

Before putting it down Audrey looked at the receiver, which is what characters do in films but seldom in life.

In the doorway was Mr Woodruff.

'You've no business in the office. You've been told before.'

'I thought it was an emergency.'

'What was it?'

'A woman. Don't tell. Nobody saw.'

'I saw,' said Woodruff.

Hill Topp was a council home and in the middle of the afternoon there was no one else about.

4

'Come upstairs,' said Woodruff.

'No.'

'You don't want me to tell madam you answered the phone. Come upstairs.'

She followed him.

'I've seen it already.'

'Then you won't be surprised.'

He stood behind the door and undid his trousers.

Audrey shut her eyes.

'You've got to look. It doesn't count if you don't look.'

'There's somebody coming,' said Audrey. 'Promise not to tell?'

But Woodruff was already doing up his trousers halfway down the corridor.

'Mrs McBryde? My name's Foss. I rang yesterday.'

'Did you leave a message?'

'Not exactly. I spoke to someone. Audrey, is it? She was helpful, only she seemed a little confused.'

It was an educated voice and not by the sound of it an elderly one, so Mrs McBryde controlled her irritation.

'I'm sorry about that. I was away from my desk. How can I help?'

Mrs Foss was enquiring about a possible vacancy.

'None at the moment,' said Mrs McBryde, though not without satisfaction. 'Hill Topp is very popular.'

'Yes,' said the well-spoken lady. 'I've heard very good reports.'

'It's a council home,' said Mrs McBryde, 'but residents pay a supplement.'

'That wouldn't be a problem,' said Mrs Foss.

'We have a choir and on special occasions a glass of dry sherry. It's less of a home and more of a club

6

and very much a community. We go on frequent trips out. Only last week we went to a local farm where they have a flamingo.'

'Just the one?'

'It's anything that keeps the mind turning over. We don't vegetate at Hill Topp. And the cuisine is not unadventurous. It's not long since we had a Norwegian evening.'

By now Mrs McBryde was well into her sales pitch, shamelessly recycling an address she had given to a carers' conference in Ilkley where news of the Norwegian cuisine had gone down a treat, though it had puzzled the residents, the general verdict being that smoked fish only takes you so far.

'It sounds delightful,' said Mrs Foss.

'Well, I have your details,' said Mrs McBryde. 'In the natural way of things we do have the occasional vacancy. I'll put you on the list. Oh, and in the event of any correspondence please note that it's Hill Topp with two p's.'

Look through the glazed door of Hill Topp House and it might be a not untypical Edwardian mansion, which was indeed how it had started. Built on the eve of the First War it was briefly the home of a prosperous mercantile family, vacated to make way for a hospital for the war wounded. Nor did the Armistice return it to normal domestic occupation, as it was earmarked for a nurses' home. Briefly a reformatory, it was once more a hospital during the Second War, with peace meaning little change when it became the property of the newly created National Health Service. Its name and lofty situation made it sought after, with its nearest neighbour Low Moor not sought after at all and something of a sink home. It was a warning to the residents of Hill Topp of a fate that could be theirs if they put a foot wrong. Hill Topp wasn't ideal but Low Moor was proof it could be worse.

'What I never understand', said Woodruff, toying with his Angel Delight, 'is why when we get to this stage they don't do the same as in Africa, namely provide you with the bare necessities, put you on one side and let you fade away.'

With no thought of talking to himself, Woodruff was in effect doing so, with those residents of the care home who were awake not listening and those who were listening mostly deaf.

'You don't know what you're saying. And we don't live in mud huts, that's why,' said Zulema, the carer.

'When I go home, Mr Woodruff, it's all tower blocks. I 'en never seen a mud hut. When Mrs Porteous asked which part of Africa I came from, I said, "Peckham", and she thought I was being cheeky. Are you finished?'

She didn't mean the soliloquy but his dinner, where the dregs of the turkey mince had congealed into what remained of the Angel Delight. Woodruff's protective hand came over his tray indicating that he still saw possibilities in this unsavoury melange, thus frustrating Zulema in her general putting the lounge to rights prior to another long and phlegm-flecked afternoon.

In the aftermath of what Mrs McBryde was pleased to call luncheon the home was hosting the monthly visit from Mr Jimson the chiropodist, currently hand-hoovering up the meagre offcuts from Miss Halliwell's toes, which were so brown she might have been chain-smoking Craven A.

'If you were famous, Margaret,' said Mr Jimson, sucking up the bits, 'I could get a good price for these on eBay.'

Miss Halliwell, not knowing what eBay was, nodded happily. 'Or,' continued Mr Jimson, 'if you were a saint' (another well-worn snatch of small talk) 'these clippings would constitute a relic.'

He moved over to Mr Woodruff. 'Saint?' said Woodruff. 'I'm the saint to put up with this place. She hasn't got that verruca still, has she? I don't want you giving it me through polluted instruments.'

'No, we've said goodbye to that, haven't we, Margaret? Your verruca, love. You'd be welcome at any lido in the land. Though you shouldn't disparage the humble verruca,' Jimson said, giving Woodruff's feet a preliminary spray. 'It's saved plenty of chiropodists from bankruptcy and got many sensitive boys off P.T. Or P.E. as it's called nowadays.'

'I was a sensitive boy myself,' said Woodruff, 'only I grew out of it. I never liked taking my clothes off. I didn't want anybody seeing my willy. Now I don't mind. Not that anybody ever does. Do I stink?'

'Not particularly,' said Mr Jimson, giving him another squirt. 'Elderly feet seldom do. Odorous feet are more often met with in youth. Old feet are dry. You've got the feet of a forty-year-old.' And like selling toenail clippings on eBay, this spurious tribute was a staple of his podiatric small talk. 'I don't mind being sprayed,' said Woodruff. 'It's washing that weakens.' He had said this last time too, though if repetition disqualified discourse little would ever be said, particularly on the geriatric front.

'Baths,' said Woodruff, 'I give them a wide berth. They come in. They like to see you bare.'

'No,' said Jimson.

'Yes,' said Woodruff.

'They're nurses,' said Jimson. 'They're professionals.'

'That's where you're wrong,' said Woodruff. 'They're not nurses for a start. They're just lasses and they've got addicted to seeing their boyfriends bare.'

Mr Jimson steered his customary middle course.

'Some of them perhaps.'

'All of them. It's on television. They keep the photos on their phones. Nobody ever saw me bare at that age. And I never saw anybody else until I was in the army. I was shy. I was at Dunkirk and I was shy.'

'I never knew you were at Dunkirk,' lied Mr Jimson. (It was a regular untruth – the old man would've been five.) 'What was it like?'

'Morecambe,' said Woodruff. 'Apart from the shooting. Very flat. Only you don't get a medal for going to Morecambe. You should, some of the times I've had there.'

Jimson was clearing up.

'I've knelt at the feet of countless women,' he said, another remark that got a regular outing. 'Men too.'

'More women than men, I'll bet,' said Woodruff, 'thanks to the silly shoes they wear. Who was it who had umpteen shoes?'

'The Queen?' said Jimson without conviction.

'No. Foreign.'

'The Queen will have had good feet,' said Jimson, 'what with all that standing she had to do.'

'Imelda Marcos,' said Woodruff. 'She was on *Desert Island Discs.*'

The oldest resident of Hill Topp or, as Mrs McBryde liked to put it, the Hill Topp community, Miss Elizabeth Rathbone, was not subject to Mr Jimson's ministrations, not on the grounds of age but 'because I've never liked being fiddled with'. Woodruff claimed to be the oldest, an assertion Miss Rathbone couldn't even be bothered to dispute and as she presided at her jigsaw that afternoon her thoughts, too, happened to be on the Queen and her coronation.

'This little fellow holding the crown was a head-master,' she said to Phyllis who was steadfastly knitting. 'Repton or Rossall, one of those places. That was before he was made archbishop.'

'Wasn't he the one who did for Princess Margaret?' said Phyllis. 'I like the one who came after him, big fellow looked a bit like God and rode a bike.'

'I just wish I could put my hand on the Duke of Edinburgh's leg,' said Miss Rathbone, roving the table. 'It's blue with a bit of purple.' Phyllis knitted on.

Mrs McBryde was wont to boast that Hill Topp had a walled garden but Mr Peckover who spent much of his day there had no time for such pretensions.

'There's a wall and there's a garden. That doesn't mean it's a walled garden.' There was also a greenhouse, every pane of which had been almost conscientiously smashed, while the asparagus still produced the occasional spear that Mr Peckover didn't think it part of his remit to harvest. Another regular find was used contraceptives, which Peckover quietly reinterred. This afternoon, though, he had come across something momentous, a battered brass cup with a bit of chain attached, all encrusted with dirt, much as Peckover was himself. There was a call from Mrs McBryde at the front door.

'Mr Peckover, will you be wanting the foot feller?'

'Not today, thank you. I think I've just found the Holy Grail.'

'Well, don't bring it in,' shouted Mrs McBryde. 'Wash it first.'

'I'm all done,' said Mr Jimson. 'Only I'm missing Mrs Vokes.'

'Violet? She'll be having a little lie-down,' said Mrs McBryde. 'She likes to give her pacemaker a rest. I'll rout her out.'

There was no response to her knock.

'This isn't like you, Violet,' said Mrs McBryde.

Nor was it, as Mrs Vokes, in readiness for Mr Jimson, had removed her tights and was lying bare-legged on the bed, only now with her eyes fixed and well beyond the reach of chiropody. Never far from her deodorant, Mrs McBryde took in the scene before giving the room an admonitory blast and slipping Mrs Vokes's charming carriage clock into a pinafore pocket. She went back to the chiropodist.

'She won't be wanting her feet doing today.'

'No?' said Mr Jimson. 'That's unlike her. I'll normally paint her toenails. She likes green.'

'I'll pass that on,' said Mrs McBryde. 'They can do it out of respect.'

A shaken Mr Jimson made his way down the drive while Mrs McBryde telephoned Grimshaw's and, though there was no hurry, the doctor.

Now Mrs McBryde is in her office, bringing her ledger up to date with the details of Mrs Vokes's unexpected departure. Her name had been Violet, a downtrodden sort of name and not one much met with these days. When Mrs McBryde had first gone in for the business of caring, names still had a certain weight and as she flicked back through the ledger she could pick out an Ambrose, a Desmond, a Winifred, besides the usual run of Janets and Mabels. Here was still the occasional Gladys, the last one having slipped on Hill Topp's lethal flags before succumbing to pneumonia. There had been Josephs too but the only ones she came across these days were children, brought in to view their aged grandparents, their name on its second time around. It would be long enough she thought before Gladys had a rerun. Mrs McBryde had had someone apply the previous week whose name was Charlene. Not a hope. As she said to Zulema, the Charlenes of this world belong in Low Moor. Their first Kevin couldn't do up his own shoelaces. So, when Mrs Foss's letter let fall that her name was Amelia, she had sailed past several earlier candidates on her name alone.

Mrs Vokes's departure postponed another, Audrey's demotion to Low Moor. That apart, her absence scarcely registered. 'I'll miss the toenails,' said Woodruff at the same time conscious that Mrs Vokes's demise represented an opportunity. There was not much to choose between the rooms at Hill Topp. Some of them had bigger windows, the rooms warm in summer, cold in winter, but not all of them had washbasins. This was a convenience enjoyed by the deceased emerald-toed lady but unshared by Woodruff who, having trailed down the icy corridor to the bathroom on winter mornings, had long dreamed of an en suite. In advance even of the funeral he had put in a plea to be transferred, only to be informed by Mrs McBryde that the Vokes room was spoken for. 'It's already allocated.'

It wasn't but the management had particular reason not to reassign it to Woodruff or indeed to anyone of the male gender. Experience had taught Mrs McBryde that give even the most proper gentleman a washbasin and the facility would end up doubling as a urinal and the room if not the whole corridor would smell. When this had been spelled out to earlier applicants, they had been passionate in their disavowals of washbasin abuse but Mrs McBryde was adamant. The room was for ladies only. And as it happened she had someone in mind, the well-spoken Mrs Foss, who had already rung again and who would pay extra for the facility.

Funeral though it was, Mrs Vokes's obsequies were far from gloomy. It was a day out after all and in the local minibus more often hired for stag and hen nights, outings on which revellers were wont to end up mooning out of the windows. Some of this merrymaking hung on and, had the current passengers launched into ''ere we go, 'ere we go', it would not have been entirely inapposite, all of them headed for the crematorium, on this occasion with Mrs Vokes but on a trip every one of them could expect to make in the not-too-distant future.

For the prisoners of Hill Topp any glimpse of the outside world brought a shaking of heads. 'That was the High School,' said Miss Rathbone. 'I taught there once. Flats now. Criminal.'

'The allotments have gone too,' said Phyllis. 'They had hens. And a goat.'

Once at the crematorium the service was brief, even brisk. There was not much that the vicar Canon Lumley could find to say about Mrs Vokes, and what little there was, he managed not to say, certainly omitting the toenails, which was all some of the mourners knew her by. Nor was he heard in anything like silence as the Hill Topp contingent, who were the only mourners, were untouched by grief and saw no reason not to chat. Mr Dyson seized the opportunity to play the crematorium piano, a baby grand on which he thumped out 'Rustle of Spring' claiming it was a Vokes favourite and the congregation gave a reedy rendering of 'The Day Thou Gavest'. Phyllis had brought her knitting whereas Miss Rathbone, at a crossroads with *And When Did You Last See Your Father?*, could have done with not coming at all. On the bus, Woodruff had managed to convince Canon Lumley that he was a particular friend of the deceased who would have wished him to be the one to press the button that sent the coffin smoothly through the ultimate curtains. Nor could he be prevented from pressing the one adjacent, which fetched it back before

Canon Lumley ('It's not a toy') regained control of the proceedings and sent Mrs Vokes to her final rest. The Canon also cadged a lift back on the pretext of making himself available for spiritual comfort and counselling to those who required it. None did and the cup of lukewarm tea Zulema had waiting for the grief-exhausted mourners was not the lavish funeral spread the Canon had in mind.

'Hooligans,' said the woman back at the crematorium as she freshened up the gladioli. 'Teenagers would have more respect.'

'It's being old,' said the caretaker. 'Pensioners. They think they own the place.'

Mrs McBryde didn't get on with the Canon or with clergy in general. All too often they considered it part of their remit to remind the residents they were not long for this world, whereas she had always found it expedient that this be something they forget.

So, left unchaperoned by the management, Canon Lumley once more fell prey to Mr Woodruff.

'Sit down, vicar. Sit down. I wonder whether you can help me.' Nobody else was talking to him so the Canon warily sat down.

'Certainly, my son. You must tell yourself that our sister has gone to a better place.'

'Couldn't be much worse,' said Woodruff. 'However, the Church being what it is, I imagine you must have come across this sexual abuse.'

'Not personally,' said the Canon, feeling the trap closing. 'I think it's more prevalent among our Roman brethren.'

'Really?' said Woodruff. 'I thought you were all at it. I was hoping for some first-hand reports. Mind you I'm not surprised, with all that incense floating about. Though your lot is as bad and you have the women doing it.'

'Doing what?'

'Officiating. Only I think I may have come in for some of that stuff as a wolf cub. Fiddling about. Interference. Taking advantage.'

'That must be a long time ago,' said the Canon. 'I should forget it.'

'How can I,' said Woodruff, 'when I can't remember it? I may have been scarred for life. There must be someone whom I can hold to account.'

'If there was interference,' said the Canon desperately, 'I'm sure I can turn up someone who would apologise and perhaps make a donation to a charity of your choice.'

'At the moment, I'm the charity of my choice.'

'If it helps,' said the Canon, 'I can always pray for you, though as it is I've got another funeral at five.' He was about to pat Woodruff's hand but thought better of it, just giving him a wan smile and hurriedly departing.

It hadn't been a bad day, thought Woodruff. They'd had a run out in the minibus. He had sent Mrs Vokes on her way and he had made the parson squirm. Life was still worth living. True, he mourned the wash-basin but somebody new was expected who might let him share.

The Canon had been lying. There was no funeral but as Lumley made his hurried and mendacious departure he was held up by a ceremony of a different kind, a procession led by Zulema, bearing a basin, towels and shampoo, and followed by a group of acolytes and the swathed and stately figure of Gloria.

Gloria had some claim to being the most glamorous of the residents. This was by dint of her hair, which she frequently asserted had never been cut and that she could consequently sit on, a feat she would happily demonstrate. Blond once, it was now white but still voluminous and free-flowing, Gloria a grand suburban sphinx. The hair was communally washed once a week with Zulema presiding in what might otherwise have been viewed as a chore but was transformed by Gloria's self-promotion into a ceremony and a privilege. Gloria was in demand outside the home, appearing with her huge hair at local community groups and a favourite at craft fayres. Not quite a freak, she was happy to pose for selfies and in return for a small fee cut the ribbon at the occasional hairdressing salon with the funds going to trichological charities.

To be invited to the washing of the hair was to be singled out as one of the elect, with these devotees bringing up the rear of the procession, and it was this ritual with which Canon Lumley had collided. Though the ceremony itself was performed under Zulema's supervision, a professional touch came from Mr Cresswell who, ever timid, gave right of way to the Canon. 'Keep up,' said Zulema. 'The water'll be clap cold.'

Though Miss Rathbone was rumoured to have travelled abroad, Mr Cresswell was acknowledged to be Hill Topp's most cosmopolitan resident. This wasn't entirely true. A plain, unassuming man, Mr Cresswell had started off with a little barber's in Morley that he had termed a salon. He didn't really believe this and nor did his customers. It was still just 'the barber's' and it was outclassed by fancier establishments that Cresswell felt temperamentally unable to emulate: if his business failed to prosper it was because Cresswell, bachelor though he was, couldn't be ... or couldn't pretend to be ... sufficiently camp. Even his inspired sale board, Scissor's Palace, didn't really do the trick and often had to be explained to his less sophisticated clients. So, in a dramatic career gear change, Cresswell sold his shop and took up hairdressing on cruise ships where the clients were mainly elderly and weren't amused by sexual ambiguity in their hairdresser or that outrageousness of which Mr Cresswell (Clive) was temperamentally incapable. Admittedly his work took him all over but since his salon had been generally deep in the bowels of the ship, he had actually seen very little. True, he had been twice round the world and had ticked off its wonders though it meant gazing on the Taj Mahal after a morning filled with ancient scurf, and the colourful cries of the vendors who besieged the boat in the Indies were lost in Mr Cresswell's case under the roar of the dryer. But if he had not had a particularly profitable career, insufficiently camp and no better at counterfeiting it, Mr Cresswell was now happy in retirement at Hill Topp as guardian of Gloria's hair. Zulema washed, Mr Cresswell dried and styled, and Gloria was grateful.

Woodruff had of course told all to Mrs McBryde, with Audrey, as the rules required, entitled to state her case before she was despatched down the hill to Low Moor. There wasn't much to say and Mrs McBryde did most of the talking, the only scarcely relevant fact to emerge, apart from Audrey's illicit answering of the phone, being that Woodruff had, not for the first time, tried to show Audrey his willy. This if anything sealed her fate but it also jeopardised Woodruff's, necessitating another visit to the office.

'You're our most senior resident. You've got a big birthday coming up. I thought I could rely on you. I thought you were my friend.'

'I know. I am.'

'What were you doing showing it to Audrey? She won't know what it means anyway.'

'I was just passing the time. They're long afternoons.'

Woodruff had always kept her informed but only up to a point. Still, as a finger on the pulse of the home, Mrs McBryde couldn't afford to lose him.

'I'll have to put it in your notes in case you do it again.'

'I won't.'

'You'll forget. You don't want to go to Low Moor as well.'

With which thought she left him.

Which is why Woodruff, normally a good sleeper, found himself lying awake at three o'clock in the morning and shouting, 'I don't want to go to Low Moor.'

There'd always been a Low Moor, all through his life. Even when he was at little school, kindly and friendly in the first years of the war, there was the threat of Armley Park, a fierce council school with male teachers and big unruly boys. He had dodged that by being evacuated, the next threat years later with the call-up and the York and Lancaster Regiment. That had not turned out to be half so bad as he'd been expecting, quite a cushy number in fact, the only danger there a possible transfer to the Duke of Wellington's Regiment who were destined for

Korea. Even when he'd ended up working for the Corporation there was a chance he might be sent to the Sanitation Department. All his life there had been the possibility of imminent relegation. Life was snakes and ladders.

Though his flashing was nowadays less than fluent, for Woodruff it came under a therapeutic umbrella, he having read somewhere (but not the parish magazine) that senior citizens owed it to themselves to keep their more shameful inclinations in trim, as whatever made the heart beat even a little faster was not to be despised. It meant what it called self-abuse but Woodruff thought that self-display came under the same category and, since this was what made his heart beat faster, it was to be encouraged. There was a problem, though, as thanks to his occasional incontinence Woodruff had been kitted out with what he referred to as 'these plastic jobs'.

Locating his penis nowadays involved a degree of delving. This he could see was wrong. There was an etiquette to indecent exposure. It must not be clumsy. And he was looking forward to the newcomer.

Mrs McBryde rapped on top of the piano with a silver napkin ring, a relic of Mr Mountford, a sometime optician.

'Now boys and girls. Drop what you're doing and meet a new friend. This is Mrs Foss.'

'Oh, Amelia, please,' said the new arrival.

'Amelia,' said Mrs McBryde. 'We've never had an Amelia before, have we?'

'Yes, we have,' said Mrs Lightowler. 'Miss Briscoe who fell down the stairs, her middle name was Amelia.'

'The one who was obese?' said another voice.

'No. You're thinking of Miss Jessop.'

'Can you play the flute?' said Mr Dyson. 'I'm short of a flautist.'

'I'm a disappointment there,' said Mrs Foss. 'Though I'd be happy to learn.'

'Too late in the day for that,' said Dyson. 'They never play the flute,' and put his earphones back on.

'You don't know anything about archaeology?' asked Mr Peckover more timidly.

'Mr Peckover's into old things,' said Mrs McBryde.

'I've been to Stonehenge,' said Mrs Foss, still anxious to please. 'Only that was years ago.'

'I don't suppose it's changed,' said Woodruff.

'I have a little museum,' said Peckover. '*Objets trouvés*. Some people might say it's a cabinet of curiosities.'

'Other people would say it's a load of old rubbish,' said Woodruff.

'Mr Dyson dreams of having a quartet,' said Mrs McBryde. 'Except that he's the only one who plays.'

'Thank God,' said Woodruff.

'That's the beauty of knitting,' said Phyllis. 'It's silent. You don't need anyone else. Only wool.'

'Jigsaws too,' said Miss Rathbone, though any fool can knit (which she didn't say).

The next day Woodruff waylaid Mrs Foss.

'Would you marry me?'

'I don't know you,' said Mrs Foss.

'I didn't say "will you", I said "would you", other things being equal.'

'What things?'

'My body, for instance. It would have to appeal.'

'It wouldn't.'

'How do you know? You haven't seen it. That could be arranged. Are you not curious?'

'No. I was in the St John's Ambulance Brigade.'

'You don't even know my name.'

'Woodruff.'

'My first name. It's Frank.'

'I can't call you that.'

'Why not?'

'It was my husband's name. I never liked it. I thought I'd heard the last of Frank.'

'Are you sure you're old enough for Hill Topp?' asked Woodruff. 'What's a sophisticated woman like you doing in a place like this?'

'Has she seen the sights yet?' said Miss Rathbone.

'Give him time,' said Phyllis. 'She's only been here five minutes. What is it today?'

'It's the Queen changing a tyre,' said Miss Rathbone. 'That was during the war when she was Princess Elizabeth.'

'What with her being in the ATS,' said Phyllis. 'When she became queen there was someone to do that for her.'

'"Do you read" and "can you read" are not the same questions.' Woodruff was persisting with Mrs Foss. '"*War and Peace*" might answer the first question and "Gentlemen lift the seat" the second. Do you smoke?'

'No.'

'Nor me. So we've got something in common.'

Mrs McBryde was opposed to both death and smoking, and while she could do little about the first she could make the second very uncomfortable. She also abhorred television, so smokers and TV fans both found themselves confined to the coldest room in the house, as what was euphemistically called The Library had its windows permanently open against the fug.

Most of the residents of Hill Topp came kitted out with an iPad, preferring to watch them (when they were not mislaid) in the comfort of the lounge. Miss Rathbone did not smoke but nor did she think an iPad anything other than a passing fad. Until TV found a way of representing jigsaws on the small screen, Miss Rathbone would not venture in The Library. She was a reader but then The Library had no books.

The exalted attributes of so many of Mr Peckover's finds were something of a joke, to the extent that these days he was careful to avoid sharing his excitement. Did another resident show a polite interest he was touchingly grateful, and so it was with Mrs Foss.

'I found this yesterday,' said Peckover, showing her a brass ashtray, from the days when Hill Topp was a nurses' home.

'It's a medieval alms dish possibly from a chapel on the site.'

Mrs Foss expressed the appropriate wonder.

'And that bundle of old canes is interesting. Towton, the battlefield, is practically next door. These would be bows held in reserve by the Yorkist army. Not needed as it turned out, which is why they've landed up here.' Mrs Foss fingered them thoughtfully. 'And something else from Towton, a fragment of Lancastrian armour, do you see how it's curved to fit the body?'

'Curved to fit the chassis, more like. It's from an old banger.'

This was Woodruff who'd seen Peckover chatting to Mrs Foss and had come out hoping he might be included. Not for him to be respectful. 'Towton seems to me a very elastic battlefield. We're thirty miles away. Any codpieces?' Peckover smiled apologetically at Mrs Foss and picking up his alms dish and his body armour stumbled back inside.

'That wasn't very kind,' said Mrs Foss.

'I'm not kind,' said Woodruff. 'I'm honest.'

'It's his little bit of romance. Haven't you any hobbyhorses?'

'I'm not barmy,' said Woodruff. 'Towton. It'll be the Somme next.'

'What did you do?'

'In life?' said Woodrow.

'Is this not life?'

'Not for me, it isn't. I'm the oldest resident.'

'So I've been told.'

It was an edgy conversation. He liked her. She didn't like him especially but she had invested what was left of her life in this institution and she needed to make it work.

'I think it's teatime.'

'Tuesday,' he said. 'Eccles cakes.'

'Could you hold my arm,' she said. 'I need help on the stairs.'

As they laboured up the stairs Mrs Foss was pleased to see a window cleaner polishing the glass on the front door. 'It's nice they look after the place.'

'Gus?' said Woodruff. 'He's never away, are you, Gus? You must be coining it.'

Gus smiled and, knowing Woodruff took no offence, went on with his polishing. He knew he made significant contributions to the happiness of the home, though it was not in virtue of his windows. In the unlikely (and quite portly) presence of its window cleaner, sex wasn't quite out of the question at Hill Topp. Far from young himself, Gus was a not atypical member of his profession and thus alert to chance encounters. Even so he had been surprised, though not shocked, to find appraising glances still to be met with here in an environment he would have thought well past it. Hill Topp was plentifully endowed with windows and in the course of cleaning them Gus had accumulated a shifting clientele of four or five customers for services that were hardly detergent. Currently he was servicing four ladies and one gentleman. Discretion was of the essence, with the theatre for these encounters an ex-bicycle shed that nowadays housed only an old lawnmower, and Gus's clients (a token sum changed hands) knew of each other but with nothing so formal as a rota. This was understandable as these days a client might not always feel up for it. Other residents could often be heard voicing relief that they were at last freed from the burden of sexual intercourse, without being aware that it was still undertaken in the cycle shed. 'Dear Gus,' as Mrs Porteous said. 'It's such a nice change from humbugs,' – a sentiment shared with Mr Dalrymple but whose requirements were more complicated.

Even when they had to cry off, Gus's coterie found their misbehaviour unexpectedly rejuvenating. After all, sex was a secret and secrets did wonders for the spirits. To be doing something so authentically disgraceful and under the nose of authority took nerve and nerve was young. Love of course would have been the real rejuvenator but whereas Mr Dalrymple did not rule it out, Mrs Porteous, even when behaving shamefully, retained a sense of social position and so thought love out of the question.

Oblivious to what went on in the cycle shed, the residents were otherwise on their toes. Things often went missing at Hill Topp and there were disagreements that were no less bitter for being over trifles. Cardigans, scarves and more intimate accoutrements like hearing aids or false teeth and even wigs. Rather than acknowledge that their disappearance might be due to absent-mindedness, the old people jumped more gratifyingly to the conclusion that they had been robbed, and as often as not by their friends and neighbours. This meant that there was seldom a time when universal accord prevailed. There were always petty quarrels, times when residents were not friends and convinced of each other's guilt. Private tiffs, simmering disagreements though mitigated to some degree by failing memory. They quarrelled but forgot who with. 'She's on the pinch is that one. I used to have a belt just that colour and now she's got it on. You can't trust anyone and I'm sure these aren't my proper teeth. I never used to have this bother.' A prolonged search for a missing jigsaw piece would convince even the eminently sensible Miss Rathbone that it had been purloined out of sheer mischief. And how explain a wig had gone walkabout when it was eventually discovered down the side of a settee?

'It's same as us,' said Mr Raybould. 'We're all lost property now.'

'I've forgotten what he looks like,' said Miss Halliwell.

'Who?'

'Prince Charles.'

That was another thing that was always going missing, what they were talking about.

'Why do you need to know?'

'I don't but it's better to be on the safe side. They're always popping in.'

'Who?'

'Celebrities.'

'I don't know why she bothers,' said Phyllis. 'Everybody knows.'

'What?'

'That it's a wig.'

'Things I'll never know,' said Phyllis, knitting away, 'my son-in-law's birthday and the location of the septic tank.'

'It'll come,' said Miss Rathbone. 'Meanwhile see if you can find a little white dog. It belongs to Mary Queen of Scots.'

More by inadvertence than larceny Mrs McBryde had accumulated a small collection of powder compacts, a compact a regular component of a deceased's effects and, wielded until the very brink of the grave as a way of giving a genteel two fingers to mortality, they were as much relics as any of the supposed artefacts unearthed by Mr Peckover. Tarnished, mostly tawdry and still redolent of ancient 4711 eau de cologne (two of them even monogrammed), they occupied a bottom drawer in Mrs McBryde's office from which she occasionally took them out to sniff and sort on an empty afternoon.

Coming upon her sifting through them, Mrs Foss was intrigued but uncensorious. 'I haven't taken them,' Mrs McBryde hastened to assure her. 'They're just stuff folks have left. You don't want one, do you?' Mrs Foss didn't. 'No, folks don't go in for powder much these days. Mr Dalrymple used to use powder with his nose though you weren't supposed to know and most of it went down his waistcoat.'

'Leave them with me,' said Mrs Foss. 'I'll do them up a bit. They might knock on somebody's box. Any other treasures?'

'I've one or two bits and bobs,' said Mrs McBryde, hauling out a battered suitcase, itself a relic of a long-dead resident. 'People leave all sorts. This tiepin is quite nice. I have to save them,' she explained, 'in case the relatives get in touch.'

'About a tiepin?'

'You'd be surprised. I kept a pair of corsets for months. Then the daughter-in-law who was into amateur dramatics turned up out of the blue and she said she could use them.'

'Medals?' said Mrs Foss.

'One or two. And there's a market for them. But they're not mine to sell.'

'What if it was for the home?'

'This home?'

'Call it The Friends of Hill Topp?'

'A tabletop sale?'

Mrs McBryde was dubious. A Friends of Hill Topp might feel licensed to make not so friendly suggestions about the way the home was run or, unthinkably, how it could be improved. Friends of Hill Topp might even suggest how the residents could have more of a say. No. The Home was better off without Friends. But Mrs Foss was not to be discouraged; she had already started accumulating.

Mr Dalrymple contributed a cricket ball. '"A corky" we used to call it. I took ten wickets with it in one match when I was fourteen. It's inscribed but you can't read it now.' Mr Raybould had some medals ... not his own and probably not even his father's but maybe of some interest. Someone else contributed a Teasmade that once had worked and might with detoxing do so again. Gloria offered to give free selfies with her hair and (though unexpectedly miserly about his accumulated treasures) Mr Peckover donated an ancient pair of false teeth ('relics of the dawn of dentistry'), which he had discovered in the foundations of the Nissen hut.

Meanwhile Mrs Foss went on with the collecting. The old people understandably clung to the few reminders of their past they had been allowed to retain . . . watches, though these days they seldom had appointments to keep, photographs not quite sepia in tone but dating back half a century and more and a sometimes necessary reminder of how they had once looked.

'That was me,' said Phyllis in an unaccustomed pause in her knitting, brandishing a snap of her paddling at Filey in the year of the Festival of Britain.

Mr Raybould matched this with one of him at Black-pool, a scrawny youth in a bathing costume, giving it to Phyllis to admire.

'Would you have fancied me then?'

'I might,' said Phyllis. 'Was that cossie hand-knitted?'

Buckles, fountain pens, tiepins, watchchains, pipes, a cigarette holder, letters, paper knives, earrings . . . there was a market for all this.

'They used to be called jumble but they've gone up in the world. These aren't jumble. They're col-lectibles.'

And the take-up was quite respectable. By dint of canvassing the sometimes reluctant residents and visiting them in their rooms, Mrs Foss put together a sizeable collection. There were the compacts to begin with, one or two of which might actually be worth money. And even Miss Rathbone found an old scent bottle, empty except that Miss Rathbone still found it redolent and so would not part with it. There were three or four watches that Mr Cartwright had got going again. There was a scarf from VE Day. Ties, bangles, some of which Gloria generously offered to model. Saddest were the photographs, none particularly ancient and many of sweethearts and young husbands in uniform from the Second War. Relics of bygone stars Val Doonican, Semprini and Vera Lynn. There was a trilby property of Mr Raybould who thought that, even at seventy-eight, it made him look a bit of a dog. Books, most of them unread and unreadable, *The Floor Covering Yearbook 1948*, *An Introduction to Watercolour Painting* and the *Leeds Civic Yearbook for Victory Year 1945*.

'It's a mixed bag,' said Mrs Foss. 'But you never know what catches people's eye.'

Most mysterious of all was a plain envelope, the donor anonymous, containing the yellowing autographs of Winston Churchill, Anthony Eden and, extraordinarily, Molotov. Nobody claimed to have contributed these but they were the only items that Mrs Foss thought might make some money. She herself had supplied a supposed Constable bequeathed by her husband that (though she had hung it up in her room) had never appealed, and to give it to The Friends of Hill Topp wasn't a wrench.

Playing no part in the scavenging was Woodruff. Whereas Mrs Foss was given unquestioned access to residents' rooms, Woodruff was a different matter, all of them knowing what would happen once the door was closed. He still had Mrs Foss in his sights but she was busy.

His frustration did not go unobserved.

'Why hasn't he shown it to us,' said Phyllis. 'What are we doing wrong?'

'Ask him,' said Miss Rathbone absently, her mind very much on her latest puzzle, Picasso's *Guernica*, which was already proving a real stinker.

The truth was, Woodruff feared Miss Rathbone with her self-possession the secret of her immunity. Unlike most of the residents of Hill Topp, Miss Rathbone didn't particularly dislike Woodruff, reminding her both in face and figure of someone she had briefly known as a young woman. Woodruff thought that Miss Rathbone liked him, and it was this that protected her and by extension Phyllis. No fun in scaring either of them. Mrs Foss and her tabletop sale was a different matter.

Not that it ever happened – or was allowed to. Race meetings went ahead. Football matches similarly. But Mrs Foss's tabletop sale in aid of Hill Topp home was summarily cancelled on account of Covid – much to Mrs Foss's disappointment and Mrs McBryde's great relief.

Mrs Foss was on her rounds, knocking on doors still seeing what she could round up, when she found a middle-aged man in the front hall.

'Is Mr Woodruff about?' (Though he was actually looking for Mrs McBryde.)

'He's about,' said Mrs Foss.

'How is he?'

'He seems very well. Are you his son?'

'Oh dear. Can you tell?'

'He's talked about you.'

Woodruff appeared at the top of the stairs.

'Don't talk to him.'

'Now then, Dad,' said the man.

'Who's your friend?' Woodruff was talking to Mrs Foss. 'You should give him a wide berth.'

'We were just chatting,' said Mrs Foss.

'I shouldn't,' said Woodruff. 'He's nothing to do with me. He comes but I don't know him.'

'Dad,' said the man.

'Don't Dad me,' said Woodruff. 'He'll be trying to get off. Does he look like me?'

'He does a bit,' said Mrs Foss. 'I picked him out as your son.'

'I've never been sure. His mam used to go over to Bradford a lot. There was a very good bus service.'

The man had a packet. 'I brought you a clean vest.'

'Does that sound like a son?' said Woodruff. 'A clean vest. A proper son would fetch grapes else flowers. A clean vest. That's a mother's job. Your mother's dead.'

'I know that.'

'Clean vest. It's my birthday. I'm about to address the company.'

'I'll be off then.'

'Stay. I don't know you. This lady doesn't know you. If this is my son, where are his papers? The first thing one would want to see would be his birth certificate. His credit card. His driving licence. I don't even know your name.'

'You do. He does. Colin.'

'Glad to have met you,' said Mrs Foss. 'Bye bye.'

'She seems a nice woman,' said Colin.

'You leave her alone. You've got someone already.'

Pause.

'How is he?'

'Who?'

'Your friend.'

'He says many happy returns.'

Birthdays were celebrated at Hill Topp without the celebrant always knowing or revealing how old they were. 'It's my birthday today,' said Woodruff, though they only had his word for it. 'As the senior resident I shall be addressing the company at noon.'

'No change there then,' said Phyllis. 'Special birthday, is it?'

'All birthdays are special at this age,' said Woodruff.

'What age?' But he wasn't saying.

'I just hope there's no talk of cake. That parkin they did for Mrs Jackson fair took the roof off your mouth.'

'Will there be any family members present?' enquired Mrs McBryde.

'Not if I can help it,' said Woodruff. 'My so-called son may put in an appearance but that's his lookout.'

Come twelve o'clock and the lounge was crowded not on account of the birthday but of the proximity of lunch that would follow. Woodruff positioned himself by the piano on which, not being a player, he struck a discordant flourish for silence. It was not wholly effective, the deaf not hearing and the rest not caring, and Phyllis remorselessly (and noisily) knitting.

'I would have thought,' said Woodruff, 'with me having achieved some seniority, you would be interested in my lessons from life.'

'Wrong,' said Zulema.

'They aren't big lessons but they often run counter to what the pundits say. The first and most important one is that there is no need to be nice. Why? Because it gets you no further. Secondly, if you drop anything on the floor don't pick it up. Why? Because the statistics of people having strokes go up the more one bends down.'

'So who picks it up?' someone asked.

'Somebody else,' said Woodruff triumphantly. 'Remember, rule one. There is no need to be nice. Similarly, if you don't want a stroke don't linger in the lav. Because that's where they happen. Don't go diddling your hands every five minutes either whatever the government says. Hygiene is overrated. Dirt never hurt anybody. I'm going to ask you another question: what famous person in history do I model myself on?'

Miss Rathbone: 'The Venerable Bede?'

'No,' said Woodruff. 'I'll put you out of your misery. The person I model myself on is Henry VIII.'

'Good choice,' said Phyllis. 'He was a card too.'

'And avoid rhubarb. You might as well drink hydro-chloric acid. These are the fruits of my experience. They're a bit sparse though there is something else while I'm on my feet. Some people still believe in God. They must be barmy. Are there any questions?'

His son, still standing by the back door put his hand up.

'Is your long life any thanks to your loving family?'

'No, it bloody isn't, as you well know. This, ladies and gentlemen, purports to be my son. It's a lie. My son is young. This gentleman is getting on.'

'We're all getting on,' said someone.

'Don't show yourself up, Dad,' said the original questioner.

'Don't Dad me. Time to call me Dad when you put me in here.'

Mrs McBryde came out of her lair.

'That's enough, Frank. Be nice. This is your birth-day, remember.' Zulema was hovering. 'And it's luncheon time.'

Going, his son knew better than to try and kiss his father but once Woodruff was busy with lunch he went in search of Mrs McBryde. Apart from the presence of Mrs Foss there had been nothing new about this encounter, which he was sometimes even amused by, but he needed to alert the management to the fact that Woodruff's stay at Hill Topp might be less permanent than the old man was assuming. His firm having, as they put it, 'let him go', he could no longer run to the home's supplement himself, and so it had fallen wholly on his son's unacknowledged friend. He needed to enquire about Low Moor.

✛

Never short of jigsaws, Miss Rathbone procured them from Age Concern, the charity shop at the bottom of the hill where they were donated along with much else by well-wishers. Selling what it could, the shop unloaded the rest free of charge on Mrs McBryde, the unwanted jigsaws being generally dull and difficult, wartime leftovers like *The Battle of Britain* (with acres of sky) and *The Battle of the Atlantic* (acres of sea). One of the blessings of jigsaws, Miss Rathbone thought, was that you didn't have to stop for lunch. They were done on a card table by her chair where Zulema knew not to put the food. Miss Rathbone ate but the work went on.

Lately, though, the supply of jigsaws had taken an unprecedented turn, Age Concern having inherited the books and residue of a retired anatomy lecturer at the university. Years ago when he was not long appointed and anxious to impress both his students and his colleagues, it had occurred to him that one means of driving anatomy into his students' heads was through play, so called. Accordingly he had transferred a complete set of anatomical illustrations, slightly enlarged . . . lung, bladder, brain, all body parts represented . . . onto boards and had them made into jigsaw puzzles. These were farmed out weekly to his sceptical students who in theory would put them together and in the process commit the intricacies of the body to the recesses of memory. That years later the jigsaws remained bright and unfingermarked suggested that as a teaching aid they had never caught on. Nor did they sell when they landed up at Age Concern and so in due course with Mrs McBryde, and Miss Rathbone, as a relief from

66

the stirring moments in the story of England, had given them a warm welcome.

Unable to envisage how the various organs could be transmuted into knitwear, Phyllis was less keen and for the moment had to fall back on producing beanies. As jigsaws the anatomical drawings were both dark and difficult, though welcomed as they had not been by the students. 'I really feel', said Miss Rathbone (she was working on *The Elbow*), 'that we are learning something.'

Phyllis ventured to disagree. 'These aren't state of the art. There'll have been medical developments since these were made.'

'On the elbow? I think that's unlikely. And say somebody falls over, as they regularly do here, I shall know exactly where a fracture generally occurs. Our jigsaw could be a lifesaver.'

❖

'Do you know what the most boring thing on television is?' This was Woodruff. Mrs Foss waited to be told. 'It's children receiving their O levels and rejoicing. It happens every year.'

'I disagree.' (This was bold in itself.) 'Some of them fail. They're disappointed.'

'Yes, only they never show them,' said Woodruff. 'Tears would do more good. A lesson learned. The sooner they get their noses rubbed in it the better.'

'In what?' said Mrs Foss.

'Life,' said Woodruff. 'Failure. You won't have come across it much, I imagine.'

'Oh, I don't know,' said Mrs Foss. 'I lost Foss.'

'That's not life,' said Woodruff. 'That's death. That's the first lesson you've got to learn.'

'This virus they're all talking about. Can you see it with the naked eye?'

Mrs McBryde didn't think so and still wasn't sure it wasn't some silliness off the television.

'It's not like nits,' said Miss Rathbone. 'It's a microbe. It percolates.'

'Does it jump?' asked Phyllis.

'You're thinking of fleas,' said Miss Rathbone, who had once done a jigsaw of a flea under the microscope.

'Morecambe's a hot spot apparently,' said Woodruff. 'No surprises there.'

The one person at Hill Topp who was not mystified by the virus was Mr Peckover. He also knew the remedy but he was keeping it to himself. They would only laugh.

Outside the government, and not always there, nobody could quite remember when people started to die. At Hill Topp the smokers in The Library might well have caught it but with the window open the mandatory six inches (Mrs McBryde's requirement rather than the prime minister's), fresh air tended to keep infection at bay. For the moment. What Mrs Vokes had died of the doctor never got round to telling the home, if indeed he knew, though since Grimshaw's embalmer was an early casualty, Covid was the assumption.

Mrs McBryde, learning that Covid concerned care homes, assumed it was care homes like Low Moor. On a hilltop for a start, at Hill Topp the wind would take care of the germs.

She continued sceptical of Covid, which belonged, if it belonged anywhere, at Low Moor. So when she herself began to show symptoms her first reaction was that it was not fair. The disease was supposed to single out old people and the occasional Asian. But she was neither. She tried to explain this to the duty doctor at the hospital and he affected to listen while entering on her record 'incipient dementia?' and arranging for a ventilator when one became available. It didn't. That wasn't fair either.

The immediate consequence of Mrs McBryde's departure was a reprieve. With Woodruff not to be trusted, all knowledge of Audrey's supposed misdemeanour went with her, thus postponing indefinitely Audrey's despatch.

Life went on with Mrs McBryde and Zulema absent, and Hill Topp continued largely unaffected. Still, the supplement had to be paid, and before she had sickened and with some reluctance Mrs McBryde had set the wheels in motion for the transfer of Mr Woodruff to Low Moor. No longer in charge herself and with no one to replace her, his demotion proceeded inexorably.

The official remedies, handwashing, social distancing and isolation, didn't cut much ice, and those lucky enough to have washbasins could count themselves doubly fortunate, though not of course Woodruff, Low Moor having no hope of an *en suite*.

Mrs Foss met Woodruff as he was waiting on the landing for his son.

'Are you packed?'

'What is there to pack? They let you have less there than they do here.'

'I shall miss you,' said Mrs Foss.

'You won't,' said Woodruff.

He began to fumble with his trousers.

Mrs Foss sighed. 'Not now. Now's not the time.'

'Now's never the time. That's what makes it the time.'

'It's nothing to me,' said Mrs Foss. 'I was in the St John's Ambulance Brigade.'

'I know. You said that last time.'

Mrs Foss relented. 'Go on then. If it makes you happy.'

She did not look away and even managed a smile.

'What do you want me to do,' asked Mrs Foss, 'cower?'

His son called up.

'Dad. The van's here.'

Woodruff didn't look at Mrs Foss, just did up his trousers, humped his bag and stumped down the stairs.

'When you say "Dad",' Woodruff said, 'does that mean I'm your father?'

'That's generally what it implies.'

And the van drove off.

Touching though this scene might seem, it was not quite the end of Woodruff. Within the hour he was back in his old room at Hill Topp and feeling as usual quite pleased with himself.

The lockdown meant that Low Moor was taking no new applicants, voluntary or otherwise, with Woodruff (the van still waiting) advised to return to his old accommodation where a new manager (Mrs McBryde still very much in hospital) would have to sort it out. Woodruff didn't make matters easier by demanding to be admitted ('I'm not having them telling me what to do'), even if it was to his disadvantage.

Typically, he presented his exclusion from Low Moor as a triumph, though Hill Topp was less than pleased to see him back and with every reason as his brief brush with Low Moor, albeit distanced, had been enough. Reluctant as ever to wash his hands every five minutes, Woodruff had carried the virus up the hill. In due course he carried it down again, following Mrs McBryde into the overcrowded local hospital.

Dying, Woodruff fancied himself wandering along the beach at Dunkirk. One of the last to get off, he seemed to be up to his waist in water, wading out to a tramp steamer that had all its lights on. He couldn't breathe but suddenly found he didn't have to as somebody began pumping him. 'That's better,' said a voice. 'Just relax' – and took his hand.

'Beats Morecambe,' he said, and died.

Most scrupulous in exercising all the precautions imposed on the public was Mrs Foss, her window always open, her hands regularly washed and with everyone at arm's length, 'though it goes against the grain as I am by nature more touchy-feely. Foss was more on the stand-offish side, social distancing right up his street.'

By dint of their long association at the jigsaw table in the window, Phyllis and Miss Rathbone constituted a bubble, as did Mr Dalrymple and Gus the window cleaner. 'Given a chance,' said Mr Dalrymple, 'I'd have bubbled up years ago.'

With Zulema now in hospital and counting herself lucky to be so, Hill Topp's doorknob went unpolished and (which impinged more) the toilets went unsquirted. While she was still at the helm

Mrs McBryde tried to remedy this, not by donning the Marigolds herself but by recruiting Gus to do the cleaning, between windows and toilets in Mrs McBryde's view there not being much to choose. Gus took a different view, feeling his status as part-time (and under-cover) sex worker might be jeopardised by him serving as a stopgap lavatory attendant. Instead, in her final contribution as Hill Topp's manager, Mrs McBryde appealed to the residents' public decency, saying the prime minister would be pleased if they were to leave the toilets as they would expect to find them, and as Zulema would have left them had she not been currently hospitalised. There was accordingly some slight improvement, not that Mrs McBryde was there to see it. She had joined Zulema in hospital, though not in the ward where Zulema was recovering but in a corridor, where she died.

✜

Those who had had the disease and lived felt themselves superior to those who had escaped it. The suffering, when there had been suffering, was assumed to have brought wisdom though it had often brought nothing of the kind, only the chance to boast. At one point, when there was a lull in the infections, it was somewhat prematurely proposed that a medal be minted, the survivors decorated, but the recrudescence of the infection put paid to that.

Even the survivors had to acknowledge that, careful though they might have been, it was a lottery, and to single them out would make no more sense than honouring the sufferings from the common cold. Calling it Common Covid would do more good. The old felt that the disease discriminated against them but disease generally does. The young felt their vigour and energy had preserved them (or most of them). What had they done to catch it after all, except breathe on one another or come together in crowds? What had they done that they would not do again? Kiss? Well, said others, we needed combing out. The world was better with fewer people. This was nature's remedy.

It was no surprise that the earliest deaths from the new disease should have been at Low Moor. Urged to distance themselves from one another, the Hill Topp contingent had space at their disposal and did as they were told, whereas the inmates of Low Moor, with no garden to speak of, could hardly help rubbing shoulders. And, gratified as Hill Topp was to fall in with the official requests, while the Cheltenham race meeting went ahead, the tabletop sale didn't. Meanwhile, microbes and viruses not yet having achieved jigsaw status, Miss Rathbone, defeated by *Guernica*, had to make do this time with *The Death of Nelson*.

Phyllis brooked no interruption to her work, though she did her best to adapt to circumstances, switching into knitting masks for the duration. However, it was complained that these were prone to permit the passage of germs, so she diversified into linen jobs, recycling some of the deceased's frocks, of which there was no shortage. Mistakenly Miss Rathbone had understood that jigsaws were banned from hospitals as infectious items, which was another reason why she determined to stay healthy. And there were still challenges. Phyllis had read somewhere of a woman who had knitted a picture of Sandringham and, having seen a photograph of W. H. Auden, her ambition, unshared with Miss Rathbone, was to knit his portrait. Miss Rathbone always implied that a jigsaw was an intellectual pursuit. A knitted portrait of the poet would put them on equal terms.

One evening Mr Peckover tentatively suggested to the few residents remaining that they make a fire, not seemingly for any reason but just to cheer them up. It was only when he had got it going and they were sat round the embers that Peckover began to talk about the plague of 1665 and how close on its heels, and seen as an act of God, had come the Great Fire of London. 'If I'd been in charge this time,' said Peckover, 'if I'd been in charge you'd have seen the back of this illness within a week. I know what is needed . . . Fire.'

With no Woodruff to disparage him and no one else inclined to, the little group hung on his words.

'Only,' Mr Peckover warned, 'the fire must be kept going. It will save our lives.'

'I like this,' said Phyllis. 'We used to call it chumping.' And chumping it was to begin with, half a dozen of them scouring the grounds for fallen branches and broken chairs, anything that would burn. Lumber. But as the sick list lengthened and more rooms fell vacant, the scope for salvage broadened, scavenging parties ranging through the empty accommodation picking up a three-legged stool here, a bedside table there, anything readily combustible.

In due course the quest began to consume more personal items. There was the late Mr Harris's flat (and greasy) cap. Mrs Hebbel's walking stick and Mr Donovan's hearing aids, about which there was some discussion. But, as Mr Dalrymple said, 'The ear is connected to the mouth and the germs come in through the mouth. Safest to burn the lot.'

Mr Hornby had been an antique dealer and it pained him to see among the combustibles valuable pieces from Waring & Gillow that had been in the house since it was built now consigned to the flames. There were half a dozen Windsor chairs condemned to the same fate and a magnificent refectory table. But if the fire had to be kept fed (and Mr Peckover insisted that it did), there could be no quarter.

London had burned from end to end. They must hold their nerve.

In the interests of hygiene they also burned the belongings of the dead and, with Mrs Porteous's shoes particularly fire resistant, Miss Holden chucked on her own windcheater and Mr Goodison's walking stick.

'I could've used that,' said Mr Raybould.

'No you couldn't,' said Miss Holden. 'It would have been full of germs.'

'A walking stick?'

'Everything. That's why we burned Mr Donovan's hearing aid. It was a death trap.'

At Low Moor the residents looked up at the bonfire and wondered what there was to celebrate.

Surveying the scene from her jigsaw table Miss Rathbone remembered seeing the glow of the Blitz in the sky. Horrifying though that as a girl had been, there was satisfaction in it. They deserved it. Bombs or no bombs England had to change.

And watching the glow of London burning night after night she had not despaired. There would be a better time. Now, she was not so sure.

Food was a constant problem. Quite early on in proceedings Mr Peckover stuck a notice on the gate,

'Food please', and with it a large flat stone to receive any offerings. This was partly, it has to be said, so that he could lay a stone similar to that used during the Great Plague. But their bacon was actually saved by Mr Parviz of Parviz Fruits on the other side of the hill. It was a shop Mrs McBryde had never used, except for the occasional bottle of milk. Now Mr Parviz was only too glad to be of service, and with a diet of curries far more varied than they had been used to pre-Covid. 'I suppose this is what you would call eclectic,' said Mr Dalrymple, 'only it's delicious,' with Mr Parviz proffering a sample pinch of spices or a surprising nut. This was society. This was fellowship.

Some of the ladies had taken Mrs McBryde at her word when years ago in her idealised picture of social life at Hill Topp she had mentioned 'the occasional tea dance'. Mindful of this possibility, and downsizing before coming into the home, the more affluent of the residents had hung onto choicer items of their wardrobe. Hartnell, Givenchy and, in the late Mrs Porteous's case, the family Fortuny. Having passed on, Mrs Porteous had left her cherished frock hanging bereaved in her wardrobe, proofed against moth but not in the eyes of her nieces against Covid. It was untouchable and thus available now to Mrs Foss and to Phyllis, who had never heard of Fortuny, just finding it (or portions of it) particularly comfortable on the face as she ransacked the house for mask materials. 'It's called improvising,' she said to Miss Rathbone, who called it vandalism but like most things kept that to herself. Ruthlessly cannibalising the ancient velvet, Phyllis got some sixty masks out of it. 'Though I've had to sacrifice the fringe,' she said as she scissored this ancient couture.

The guidance from the government hardly seemed relevant. Isolated they already were and now masked thanks to Phyllis diversifying with whatever came to hand, ranging from Dior to Balenciaga to what remained of ancient vests.

With Mrs McBryde gone there was something of embarkation leave to life now. Advancing in years and sober in inclination, the surviving denizens of Hill Topp seized their moment and for what little time might be left to them they frolicked. This chance might not come again. Arthritis permitting, they scampered. It helped that it was warm, the sun loosened stiffened limbs and brought a return to fluency.

There would come a day when the nation was excused funerals and what went too was some sense of the ridiculous, Mrs McBryde having been the line they had had to tread. Now she had gone, Covid had given them the chance to be something else.

The survivors weren't always the best informed.

'I miss going to the pictures only you're not allowed now.'

'And you never went before.'

'I went before I came in here.'

'Church too.'

'Can you not go to church? Not that I ever did much.'

'Singing broadcasts it apparently.'

'What?'

'The germs.'

'And kissing. Singing and kissing.'

'In my time it was TB.'

'Only this is still our time. And there still is TB in some places apparently.'

'I suppose you can't have sex with it either. No singing, no praying, no sex.'

'You can have sex if you're in a bubble.'

'Where do you get them?'

'What?'

'These bubbles.'

'It's more of an expression.'

'What about bingo? Can you have that?'

'No. It's anywhere you breathe the same air. Bingo's the same as church.'

'It never is. It's the opposite.'

There was a pause.

'What happened to your sister-in-law's pet shop?'

'That's in abeyance. It has to be else they jump on you.'

'What else do you miss besides the pictures?'

'I forget.'

'People?'

'No. I miss the sea.'

'The sea?'

'Coming in and going out.'

That these half a dozen old people were ultimately able to hang on in their residence relatively undisturbed and to the despair of the authorities was entirely due to luck. When Covid put paid to Mrs Foss's tabletop sale, she was left with a heap of jumble. Mrs Foss had thought to house it in her own room for safety's sake but reflecting that now most of the donors had fallen victim to the virus, while being unaware of the place's dubious associations, Mrs Foss transferred the putative collectibles to the bicycle shed, in doing so becoming convinced that Woodruff had been right in thinking it rubbish. Even her husband's cherished landscape looked less promising than it did when hung on her wall, so that too was consigned to the shed.

Gus the window cleaner, who still misused the location from time to time, could hardly complain and in any case the bric-a-brac scarcely got in the way of sexual activity. Not that there was much of that these days with the only survivor of the original clientele, and that sporadically, being Mr Dalrymple.

His faltering ardour was fed by the perusal of some ageing pornography donated by Gus as part of the service, though having been an art historian Dalrymple was somewhat superior about this material. 'I suppose it makes a change from *The Burlington Magazine*.'

Cut to one sunny afternoon when Gus and Mr Dalrymple were busy in the shed. It was hot and Gus had Mr Dalrymple jammed up against Mrs Foss's mountain of junk. Out of courtesy Dalrymple was reckoning to peruse one of the magazines but since it was the same one as Gus had supplied at their last encounter it was slow doing the trick. It was at this point that the sun forced its way through Gus's uncleaned windows to rest upon Mrs Foss's grubby and painted cloud. Disengaging himself ('This won't take a moment'), and with his trousers round his ankles, Dalrymple stood up.

'Have you got my spectacles?'

'What the fuck for?' Still, Gus finds them and now equipped with his glasses Dalrymple shuffles across the floor, trousers down, to ease Mrs Foss's picture from the surrounding junk. Opening the shed door, he holds the picture up to the light and almost has the climax Gus had been so slow in providing him. Spitting on his fingers, he rubs his hand over the varnish to confirm his suspicions.

'I think this might be a Constable.'

'So what?' said the otherwise occupied Gus. 'It isn't against the law. It hasn't been for years.'

95

'Foss always swore it was,' his widow said later. 'To my shame I never really believed him.' Now, not quite post-coitally and still in his underpants, Dalrymple believed him. And so indeed did Sotheby's and the art world generally and to the satisfaction of the estate agent from whom, with the proceeds, the survivors purchased the lease.

There remained Miss Rathbone.

Miss Rathbone had always kept herself to herself, never sharing her previous life with the other residents, even Phyllis, her reticence to some extent a consolation in her loneliness. She was not taciturn by choice, though. Scarcely out of her teens she had been put under a vow of silence, forbidden to tell her secrets before she had known she had secrets to tell. A clerk at Bletchley Park, she had signed the Official Secrets Act, the secrets military not personal though Miss Rathbone had chosen to make her vow personal as well as professional, applying it to the remainder of her life . . . and it had been a remainder, with nothing as absorbing or as exciting happening to her in the long years since. Girls she had known were not so discreet and as Bletchley began to figure in films and plays and reminiscences, Miss Rathbone found herself despising these renegades still under the same prohibition as she was.

Now ill in bed, U-boats slid through her dreams, haunted as they were by oil-soaked sailors drowning in the North Atlantic. Morse code too she heard in the next room.

'Am I dying?' she said to Phyllis.

'Dying?' said Phyllis. 'Let's get old age out of the way first.'

It crossed Miss Rathbone's failing mind that in spilling the beans at this late juncture she was breaking the habit of a lifetime and doing exactly what was expected of someone who was at the far end. Better die as the enigma she had always been. Except that the truth was more interesting. Having incubated her memories for most of her life, perhaps now was the time to speak.

She was in bed and at her bedside Phyllis who for once had put aside her knitting.

'Did you do something wrong?'

'It didn't have to be wrong. You weren't supposed to talk.'

'Who to?'

'Anybody. Mum. Only I met somebody. I was young. It was in the war. I went abroad. I was picked to go. I was good at my job.'

'Typing?'

'Not typing. Deciphering. I once had to take some decoding to a bunker in Whitehall. To Churchill. I put it in his hands.'

It occurred to Phyllis that this might be the start of dementia.

'Where abroad? France?'

'It wasn't France. It was somewhere called Yalta. On the Black Sea. It's a resort, only it's not Blackpool. They were having a conference. Look in my cupboard.'

Phyllis did as she was told.

'There's a little black box.'

'No. Not that. That's just a brooch.'

'There's a scent bottle.'

'That's it.'

'It's empty.'

'I know. Only it still smells. Mrs Thing wanted it for her jumble sale but I wouldn't give it to her.'

'Why?'

'It still smells.'

'Only just.'

'Put it to my nose.'

Phyllis cast aside her knitting and did as she was told.

'French, is it?'

'No. Nothing's French.' Miss Rathbone sniffed though it turned into a cough. 'It's Russian. Soviet anyway. It was this high-up in the Soviet delegation. Said it reminded him of his wife. I never liked it much but he took a shine to me and made me wear it. We both did.'

'Was she dead, the wife?'

'No. Just in Moscow. She was the head of the state perfume department.'

'Do you know his name?'

'Course I know his name. Everybody knows his name. Molotov.'

'Oh,' said Phyllis. 'Like the cocktail. Was he a nice man?'

'Not really. He smelled nice. He was like Woodruff. Nobody liked him but me.'

Miss Rathbone tried to sigh but it became another cough.

Phyllis waited. 'I'm listening.'

'Don't listen,' said Miss Rathbone. 'Just let me tell you . . . He liked me. I knew just from the conference room. He wasn't anything special but then nor was I. We had to be very careful from his people's point of view as well as mine, only one of our delegation picked up on him being sweet on me, so they got me to push it a bit just to see what transpired. He always wore braces . . . suspenders the Americans call them.

He always wore scent. This scent . . . There you are,' she said, plucking at the sheet. 'That's my secret.'

'Do you feel better for telling me?' asked Phyllis.

'Not really,' said Miss Rathbone. 'I just feel lonely. The only other person I met was Alan Turing. I knew that wasn't going anywhere either. He wept on my shoulder.'

'So you had a life,' said Phyllis, picking up her knitting.

'He learned a joke. Afterwards, when I was going, I would say, "See you later, alligator", and Molotov would say, "In a while, crocodile."'

Stories often end with a wedding but one imagines that residents of care homes seldom marry. It's a bit late in the day and anyway the only couple left in the story who could conceivably wed are Mrs Foss and Mr Peckover and they've both got more sense.

Still, one should tidy up and so in one of its several lulls, Covid now permitting church services while at the same time thinning the congregations available to attend them, Miss Rathbone dies . . . found by Phyllis with her fingers still cradling an errant piece of an uncompleted jigsaw. At her funeral there was a discreet as ever revelation that she had been awarded the CBE, the brooch in the little black box on the coffin. Then to finish with, as she had stipulated, there was a recording of the 'all-clear'.

AN APOLOGY

Lest it be thought that Madame Molotov (Polina), a leading light in Soviet cosmetics, is a figment of my imagination, she comes from an article by Sasha Raspopina that appeared in the *Guardian* (19 November 2014, first published in *The Calvert Journal*).

Familiar to the public more from the eponymous cocktail than his unyielding diplomacy, Molotov's hinterland deserves to be more widely known and it seemed a pity to leave this sweet-smelling incongruity unexploited. And who is to say that, no slouch in the field of international relations, Molotov should not have enjoyed a bit on the side.

Alan Bennett